Short Stories and Conversations

ISBN: 9798500124470

DEDICATION

This book is dedicated to my wife, Grace; she
gave her life and made me a better man

CONTENTS

Acknowledgements

I would like to thank Beverley for her invaluable assistance in enabling the publishing of this book. Without her help, nothing would have come to fruition.

Foreword

We have created these short stories and conversations through inspiration and ability, which depict imaginary events portrayed through somewhat ordinary events and people, some with rather extraordinary results.

We trust you'll enjoy reading these stories as much as we enjoyed writing them.

THE BOARDROOM

The vast marble edifice stood high and intimidating against a clear blue sky and strangely compatible with the garden setting, which had reached full maturity in a few short years. The dingy structures on all sides mocked the skyline contrast, the elegance of this high-rise building. Without a doubt, this building was a truly magnificent creation and lasting memorial to the genius of Sir Robert Dodswell, president of the Royal College of Architecture. On this beautiful July morning, the human tide of workers was making their way into London.
Most travelers had long since become immune to the local landscape, being solely bent on arriving at their predestined destinations with as little fuss as possible. But, entirely at peace with the world around stood a gardener.

He was dressed in a green oversized faded uniform, filthy boots, and a grey cap with Earl embossed. Earl was more than ready to face the day filled with beauty all around him. Early as usual, with a peaceful expression hidden from the rest of the world, which seemed to be speeding past.

He was engrossed in his labor for the day since he was tending to his beloved roses, which once again were cluttered with the excesses of the previous night's revelry in the form of discarded takeaway cartons, greaseproof papers, and other unmentionable objects discarded by the younger generation after the previous night's activities.

They had invaded the grassed areas. He was a brilliant man, and he often wondered what made him carry on with this humble activity.

Earl could forgive all the routine excesses, but the "scuff" marks on his priceless imported sea-washed turf and the unmentionable plastic objects routinely hurt his sensibilities.

He realized that the generation gap and his strict moral upbringing did not help deal with his perceived disrespect for nature.

It was evident to anyone conversant with the

regular comings and goings that the arrival of a fleet of cars and taxis outside the main entrance of the building had to have some important significance.

It was, in fact, the meeting of the executive committee of the English Elevator Company at their Head Office in London. The elevator company was a household name and was known locally as the 'Big E".

Entry into the Head Office's center of excellence involved stringent security checks before the unrecognized individual could proceed onwards.

The immediate impression was one of twentieth-century luxury and efficiency. The lack of any noise, other than the bell denoting the arrival of one of the elevators, was most noticeable. The ride in the elevator was always impressive, mainly due to the lift being constructed on the outside of the building and constantly being modified to keep up with the latest technical developments.

Gliding upwards to the tenth floor took only seconds.

The fall in the ambient temperature was immediately noticed on departure into the corridor adjacent to the Boardroom. It was said that the temperature setting helped heighten the level of uncertainty and anticipation of the delegates, which was very much akin to the role of the slaves before encountering the lions in the Roman Forum.

Within ten paces of leaving the elevator and directly ahead was the venue for the executive management committee, and visible was the sign highlighted as 'Meeting in progress.'

At this meeting, all the major divisions of the organization were represented. Sitting at the head of the long mahogany table sat Cyril Watson, the Group Managing Director, a relatively lean individual, who at 55 years was regarded as a high-flyer in the worldwide organization.

Watson was not noted for the subtlety of his conversation and had been brought to the United Kingdom operation from the United States to redress the recent appalling and rapid decline in the business performance of the United Kingdom operation. On Watson's right stood George Harrison, the Group Financial Director who was about to begin presenting the financial results. The rest of the committee was made up of Joe Bailey, a handsome-looking American whose robust management style did not easily lend itself to his executives. It was said that Joe could not be underestimated because of his good looks and that he had once fought a wild boar in a one-to-one contest and had won. While most did not accept this tale, others readily believed that this could be true. Joe had brought along his financial advisor Barry Hughes to ward off any delicate questions.

Sitting right next to him was Richard Watson. Richard was by far the most extinguished-looking male in the room. He was a typical English manager who, at the age of 35 years, had all the drive and imagination needed to reverse the dramatic decline in his division's fortunes.

He had come alone because he was highly numerate and was more than able to comment on any financial matter.

The rest of the group consisted of two substantial businesses. Both Managing Directors and their financial advisers were sat on the opposite side of the Boardroom table to emphasize their distinction. There was a bond between these two teams, but this was mainly a self-help form of allegiance at the Board level only.

Shamus O'Toole represented the Irish division, a most erudite and scathing man when the chips were down and the most charming individual when in need. His accomplice was a shifty-looking character whose razor-sharp brain had enabled the Irish division to achieve results that were the envy of the rest of the group and therefore made meetings a most relaxed affair for them.

Lastly and most vulnerable was John Miller, a robust-looking man of heavy build who would look good on any rugby or sports field.

Miller was a self-educated man, and his intelligence gave him the edge amongst all his colleagues: perhaps in an English sense, his major drawback was that he had been born too far north of the Thames.

Miller's financial Director was a somewhat effeminate man named Vincent Underwood, who sat in a crouched position to appear as invisible as possible. His stated objective was to obtain a well-remunerated position in complete obscurity.

But unfortunately, he had not yet reached such an

exalted level.

George Harrison had recommended his presentation of the financial results of the last month. He had most of the salient points with the use of an overhead projector and well-defined graphs. The audience listened to the latest horror stories and waited for expedited for Cyril Watson's response. Watson sat, looking blankly ahead as if stupefied by Harrison's monotonous tones.

To the onlooker, it might have appeared that he did not hear the same message that the rest of the audience was hearing. Harrison hesitated in his delivery for a split second. To everyone's complete amazement, Watson jumped from his seat as if stung by a hornet and facing Harrison directly. He commenced uttering the most vitriolic tirade that had been heard in the history of these meetings. "Jesus Christ,

Harrison, I have now been Managing Director of this group for almost one year, and you still trot out the same old sad story!"
"Boss, the situation is not improving. On the contrary, we are going into ever deeper waters. So, naturally, our European Headquarters will be most displeased."
"Do you know something" continued Watson
"I cannot believe the numbers you are sticking up

on those slides. I came into Europe as the savior and not as some bloody half-witted prophet who can't manage the numbers game."

Pausing for a moment and waiting until he knew his audience was captured, Watson modulated his voice, and in menacing tones, he addressed Harrison "I had a dream last night, and in this dream, you were telling me that the profit was good, that the future was bright, and that we were the toast of the whole worldwide organization, and toward the end of your statement, I woke up and found that I had wet the bed."
"God only knows what I am going to tell my wife Katie tonight."
Joe Bailey, who had known Watson for many years and attended many meetings with him, had been enjoying this operatic scene, injected with "Boss, I would tell Katie that the Persian cat crapped on the bed in a moment of ecstasy; when you were stroking it."
"Ah, very clever Joe," responded Watson, and the look that passed between the two lifelong friends was positively hostile and served to make Joe realize that all was not well. Meanwhile, Harrison, who by now was visibly shaking, had dropped into his seat like a boxer

who had gone one round too many.

Watson looked at his team and said, "Understand me, I am telling you the truth.
You had better believe it. We are all for the high jump if we don't pull this group around. Harrison had worked long enough with Watson to realize that this man was not joking, and he dreaded to contemplate the future working with him.
"Okay, George," continued Watson, let's get down to business.
Shall we start at the beginning by analyzing what has gone wrong, or better still, let us consider what has gone right."
For reasons unknown Harrison, again stood up and addressed Watson like a schoolboy answering the master.
"Well, boss," he said in a high pitched, whining voice, "it is not easy for me to say what has gone right with the month's results, output from all our manufacturing units has dropped, and our service departments and installation teams are not performing very well, these problems allied to our high fixed costs-structure is giving us continuous bad results."

"Bravo, bravo," responded Watson. Those remarks were the most profound statements that we were all waiting for; based upon this information, I am sure we can all pull the ship off the rocks.", was the mocking reply.

"I am sure that we are all amazed at the glibness of your statements, not a word is new, next month, don't bother coming to the Board meeting, just send us a tape, and we will play it over.", responded Watson.

Just as Harrison was digesting this latest public admonition, he glanced down to his papers. He realized that the bombshell he had to bring to the Board's attention was still under wraps.

Realizing that this was not to be one of his more successful meetings, Harrison looked down the length of the table. He said, "Oh, the way, Boss, I was told just minutes before the meeting that we have an accounting error of over one million pounds. The good month that we thought that we had last month was due to a computer input error by one of our clerks, and we must correct this next month."

There was an audible gasp from most of the Directors, but Watson's expression did not change at all.

Then, finally, Harrison looked over to where Watson was sitting, and in a hushed tone, he said, "Boss, are you alright? You look as though you are switched off?"
"Switched off," mumbled Watson, who by this time was shaking his head as if in disbelief. "I wish that we were living in the days of ancient Rome, and I could have that little clerical bastard hung, drawn, and quartered, or fed to the bloody lions." "How can such a thing happen" injected Barry Hughes, realizing that this was probably an opening he should not miss. However, Watson was entirely oblivious to any noises within the room and leaning forward. He could propel his seat backward and walk over to the large window, which extended the entire length of the Board room.

Looking down, he was able to see the gardener still tending to the roses. The steel grey eyes of this eminent business leader remained fixed on the inferior below, and the immediate desire to change places was his innermost thought.

If only I could prune roses, for the rest of eternity, was the uppermost thought as Watson again returned to the real world, which was causing him so much anguish in the depths of his stomach.

This interlude had taken only two to three minutes. Still, it was sufficient time for all to realize that history was in the making. Harrison, who had been playing with his calculator, was waiting for the onslaught to continue. As his gaze encountered his leader, he knew that barring a miracle. He was nearing the end of the line.

Silence remained for what could only be described as eternal until finally, Watson addressed the meeting with, "Gentlemen, we have all heard the news, and it is now my turn to ask for your help and advice.

I spoke to our lords and master in Pari not less than two hours ago, and my message was that we were, at last, coming out of the forest.

"Some forest, eh, perhaps I should pick up the phone now and say Pierre Le Blanc; Pierre do you know that I said that we are, at last, coming out of the forest, well, unfortunately, we have been savaged by this big brown bear to the tune of over one million pounds.

"Do you think he has got that sense of humor!" lamented Watson. "Well, lads, what do we say?"

Predictably, Miller was the first to respond, "I cannot believe this information. We have got to think our way out of the mess."

Seeing that no one else was going to volunteer advice, Watson turned to Harrison and said, "George. I think it is fair to say that you are in the mire deeper than anybody and working on the premise that the thoughts of an empty belly clear the mind. So, I would ask you to get your big fat backside out of here and come back in two hours-time with a more interesting story."

Harrison jumped from his seat, banging his thigh bone on the side of the heavy mahogany table as he turned to leave the room. Come back with a more exciting story was his brief. The pain from his thigh bone was a pleasant relief to the anguish that engulfed his mind. His one desire was to race down the stairs and leave the problem and the company well behind.

However, common sense prevailed, and as Harrison approached his office, he could see the dim outline of someone working inside. Nodding to his secretary as he passed, he encountered Dave Smith, busy shuffling through papers on his desk.

"What do you want, Smith?" snapped George Harrison, "and what are you doing in my office?"
Dave Smith was one of the most conscientious types ever to work for English Elevators plc. and with his nervous nodding and twitching demeanor, he replied, "Well, I was just looking for my work paper on the million-pound error, have you got it, Mr. Harrison?"
"Dave, do you know that today has, up to now, been the worst working day of my entire life? Promise me that the error is not correct. "

"Mr. Harrison, the error is not right" responded Smith. "Thank God for that!" moaned Harrison "what should it be?",
"Well, Mr. Harrison, the clerk who is responsible forgot to include some other obvious costs, and it should be nearer to one and a half-million," stammered Smith. Harrison dropped down into his seat and hit his thigh collided with the table. The pain was almost a consolation. Immediately he had left the room, and he had a compulsion to run out of the building and disappear and join a monastery. Joe Bailey was never known to miss an opportunity. He knew that the situation was tailor-made for him at that precise moment.
"Cyril," said Joe, "I suggest that you don't feed any of that statistical crap to our holding bosses but

rather change the ball game, tell them what our new plans are."

" Eureka," shouted Cyril Watson thrusting his arms towards heaven and shouting, "at last the Messiah has arrived, and Bailey gives us the message; we are pilgrims on the search for the truth."

Joe knew that Cyril was extracting the urine from him but was more than ready to play his trump card, Boss, Ok Boss"

"tell them that we have started a restructuring plan, and the savings will match up."

"Sounds good," said Watson "tell me more."

"Cyril," said Joe, "get Leonard Cryton, your Personnel executive, up here and tell him that you need to know what his strategic cost reduction plans are for this year. Not only will you put him behind the eight balls, but you must get a positive response."

"Good idea", responded Cyril. Watson picked up the phone and said to his secretary, "Tell Fatzo to come up here at once. I need to talk to him."

"Who?" asked his secretary.

"Oh, sorry," said Watson to his secretary, "I mean

the learned Leonard Josiah Cryton."

The phone was hardly replaced when the main boardroom door shot open, and in came the most disgraceful human medical specimen of a man, Leonard Cryton, had arrived. He took about four steps into the room and collapsed into a rather long and wide settee.

The physical mass could be seen moving up and down rhythmically. The size of his uncontrollable belly was stretching the front of his trousers and clearly showing was his zip.

His body overflowed over the side of the settee, and his face was contorted in agony caused by everyday movement.

"You called Boss," said Cryton, "Yes", said Watson. "You took your time getting here" was the added sarcastic comment. Cryton looked over at Watson with a pathetic and subservient face,

"What can I do for you, Boss?" asked Cryton.

"Just stand up and write on the flipchart what your cost reduction plans are for the next year, "instructed Watson.

"Oh yes, sir," responded Cryton, "I am currently working on that, Sir, and I will have some answers within one-or-two weeks." But, unfortunately, the audience had already witnessed the crucifixion of Harrison, and this additional sacrifice was inevitable.

"Good Jumping Jesus," shouted Watson, "am I to be pursued to my grave by an overweight Nancy Boy."

"How long have you been troubled with your ears."

"Did you not hear what I said"

"Get up off your fat arse and write on that bloody flipchart, right now, the answer to my question."

Then, slowly but surely, Cryton started to weep, to the total embarrassment of all the onlookers.

Then, seeing that he was no longer in control of the situation, Watson adjourned the meeting to the afternoon.

Cryton shuffled out of the office, down the stairs, and proceeded to clean out his desk. He knew that Watson was unforgiving and that he had reached the end of the road.

Later that evening, after a few stiff whiskies, Cryton wrote to Watson a most forthright statement outlining his feelings towards him and his company ethics. Between the hours of 7 pm and 6 am, the body of Cryton inhaled a lethal dose of carbon dioxide from his car in the garage. Before the abandonment of the meeting, Harrison asked Smith if he wouldn't mind leaving the room.

Smith flashed through the door without a moment's hesitation.

Left alone with his thoughts, he knew that Smith was always right.

So much for the 'better story theory,' why was fate so cruel as to deal him this second blow? For once, George knew that the entire story had been revealed, at least for this moment.

Desperately trying to assemble his thought processes proved extremely difficult. Still, like many of life's tragedies, the show had to go on. Most accountants have a sixth sense, with a survival instinct, and Harrison was no exception to the rule. Firstly, time was needed to massage the problem, so therefore it was necessary to change the ball game.

Harrison's thoughts turned to the noble cause of assassination. Yes, that was it. We must get rid of people; we are top-heavy. The more he thought about the idea, the more he liked it.

He knew that he could not return to face Watson without some crumbs of comfort.

The actual mission for the Company must be restructuring. But, everyone would agree, divine providence had intervened and come to his aid.

Feeling much more composed, Harrison retraced his steps back to the monthly meeting.

When he arrived in the room, he was mildly surprised to find nobody present, except for the occasional secretary flitting around refilling the water jugs or leaving messages for delegates to read on their return. Slowly, one by one, the various directors entered the room, and the usual small talk resumed until Watson arrived some five minutes later, stumbling through the doorway; it was evident that the whisky bottle had received some treatment. "Right gentlemen, we will now listen to George Harrison's better story, over to you, George."

Harrison's confidence suffered a momentary

lapse as he stood up, but he knew that now was not the time for the faint heart.

"I have given the matter some careful consideration, and I think that I can recommend to this Board a strategy that we can all accept." Harrison continued, "I think that what we should tell Paris is first the good news, and then filter in the fact that we need to adjust our figures downwards for the past months' error." Watson looked incredulously at Harrison and grunted, "George, if I didn't know you better, I would now doubt your sanity."

"Please, please, give me the good news before I piss myself again," shrieked Watson.

Harrison was not thrown off balance. Watson was almost demented in his approach, and inwardly Harrison felt inclined to run from the room away from the problem.

Regaining his composure Harrison, coughed nervously, and said, "What we should do is tell Paris all about our restructuring plans, how we plan to save four million pounds in the next financial year, and then we can say that we wish to use some of these savings to provide from possible losses," looking sheepishly at Watson he said, "What do you think Boss?" It was immediately apparent that the sheer audacity of the plan impressed Watson, mainly because he did not make any immediate reply.

Finally, Cyril Watson, who has remained relatively silent throughout the morning's proceedings, said, "I will back that idea. Sounds good to me.", various mutterings of approval resounded throughout the room.

Meanwhile, Watson, who had remained seated, said, "George, I like the idea. After all, that's what we plan to do anyway, but we will have to phone through to Paris today. So how should we put it over?"

"No problem, Boss," said the now confident Harrison.

"I will speak to Pierre Le Blanc and say that you have gone out with one of our most important customers, but that you will ring him on Monday with a more detailed summary of our plans".

"Agreed" was the response, "that will give us three days to put the meat on the skeleton."

Joe Bailey sensed that events at the meeting were moving onto topics less dangerous. However, he reminded Cyril Watson that it would be essential to involve the Personnel department, which was not presented in the room.

"Good point," remarked Watson, and with that, he picked up the phone, which was answered immediately by his secretary. "Call Fatso to join us here immediately, Sarah".

"Sorry, Mr. Watson, who did you say?" was the predictable response. "You know who I mean, get our Director of Personnel immediately."

"Certainly, Mr. Watson, I will ask Mr. Henry Smith to attend right away."

Hardly had the phone been replaced when the Board room door shot open and in galloped Henry Smith, to say that the man was of immense proportions was, if anything, an understatement. He possibly weighed 25 stones, and his chest was heaving as though about to burst all the buttons on his shirt.

Henry made his way to the unique chair, which was set apart from the table and dropped down with an excellent flopping movement. His portly figure was distorted in the chair, and the flies on his trousers looked ready to burst. There is evidence of cannibalism within every organization at the highest levels, and Mr. Henry Smith had

long been in 'the pot.'
Watson sensed that his audience now needed some relief from the severe mood, and with this in mind, he addressed Smith.

"Henry, we have taken a decision here today to restructure our organization, our overheads are out of control, and we think that pruning is vital. What do you think?"
"Yes, Sir, I agree," replied Henry Smith, "I have had my department looking into this problem for some considerable time."
"Good," replied Watson, sarcastically, "then you should have little difficulty in presenting to me a logical and coherent redundancy plan by Monday next to that I can inform our beloved brothers in Paris of our plans.
I want to get your best men on this project and give it all you have," reiterated Watson.
"Have you got the message, Henry?"
"Indeed, I have, Sir," responded his obedient servant.

"I will call my team together on Monday next, and within two weeks, we should be in good shape to come up with an outline plan at least."

This response somewhat dumbfounded the assembled audience.

Watson, whose brow was creased into five or more deep furrows, with the veins in his neck bulging, obviously could not believe what had been said.

With the minimum fuss, Watson got up from his seat and strolled over to where Smith was sitting, and looking down on Smith, with his face about inches apart, he said, "Are you trying to take the piss out of me, Henry or have all of the slates blown off your roof."
Why, what I have said, that upsets you so much?" groaned Smith.

"You must not have been listening to the brief that I have given you, I don't want an answer in two weeks, but next Monday, got it, Smith."
"Oh, right, sir, Monday it will be."
The day's drama had taken its toll on all present, and when Watson said, "The meeting is closed, "the exit from the room was almost a stampede.

When Watson arrived home that evening, his wife, Katie, was waiting for him. "Evening, darling. Have you had a good day?" In response, Cyril responded by stating that it was probably the worst day of his entire life.

Katie said, "that is very sad, I think it is going to get even worse on two counts," Cyril responded "that is impossible, tell me the worst," Katie replied by telling Cyril, "I received a phone call from the police informing me that Leonard Cryton had committed suicide and they want to talk to you about a suicide note".

"Oh, dear" responded Cyril, "that is a real tragedy".

Cyril dropped into an armchair, absolutely shattered by the news. "What is the other news. "

"I think that you have had enough bad news for today, so perhaps we can find the reason for the need to replace the bedsheets later".

The following day the meeting continued.

Watson relayed the information that Leonard Cryton had died, and the police wanted to interview him to discuss the suicide note left by Cryton.

The delegates remained silent at receiving such terrible news.

Cyril said that he would be attending the police station as soon as this meeting ended. However, it was decided out of respect for Leonard Cryton to postpone this meeting. Watson immediately drove to the Police station, and he was interviewed by Clive Winch, one of the senior detectives.

Winch showed Watson the suicide note left by Cryton.

The note said that the bullying and interrogation techniques used by Watson and others in the organization and his marital difficulties made life too difficult to go on. When Watson read the document, he said that "he could understand that Leonard was under severe pressure to perform while also weathering marital problems. Clive Winch said that the police would not be taking any further action, but they felt obliged to notify Watson of the note's contents. Returning to his home, he realized that his wife was visiting her sister. He went immediately to the whiskey bottle, and his mood changed to one of self-interrogation.

Finally, after maybe two hours of meditation, he decided to change his ways and change his current job.

On the return of Katie from the shops, he related his latest meeting with the police and his need to change his lifestyle.

He said to Katie, "While you have been away, I have entered into a long conversation with myself, and I have experienced the most beautiful epiphany. I now totally understand the gospel of the epiphany.

Maybe my experience is insignificant compared to Paul on his road to Damascus, but I am sure that it is authentic."
Katie gave her husband a very quizzical look, and he could see that she was utterly shaken. This moment took possession of both, and they embraced with an avalanche of tears coming from Katie.

They both sat down, keeping their embrace. After a few minutes, they looked at each other, and a smile turned into another embrace.

Cyril said, "we have been living through a self-induced nightmare, and I have decided that we shall take a long holiday and afterward we will determine our future, thankfully we have got many opportunities and as they say fortune favors the brave"

Cyril explained to his management team that he had decided to retire from his current position.

The reason for his action was brought about partly because of the untimely end of Leonard Cryton. He said that he would be writing to Head Office stating that a lot of the pressure that people were working under was caused by irresponsible head office personnel who did not understand what it is like working at the coal-face".

THE END

THE WONDER BOY

George Francis (Jnr) was awakening from a profound sleep. He was conscious of a slow monotonous droning sound which he quickly established was the predicament that a bumblebee had encountered with the net curtains of his bedroom. He eventually reached consciousness and decided to come to the assistance of the hapless bee.

Slowly unraveling the curtain and opening the window, the bee was able to escape back into the wide-open world. Just before the bee flew away, it hesitated on the window ledge and looked at George.

The bridge between a creature and a human was breached. The sense of satisfaction that this brief encounter gave to George was enormous.

Lying back in his bed, he wondered how it could be that such a simple act was having such an uplifting feeling of happiness, and he certainly would like more of it.

Little did he know it, but this tiny event was to change his life forever. The complete story to date of George Francis Pardew was one of unparalleled success. He was born in the age of the computer revolution.

His father was a lawyer who did not appreciate that the world was changing and did not have the mind to try and keep up to date with progress, so it was quite a surprise that his son joined the ranks of the modern generation and opted to become a student of computer programming.

George Francis was a sensational student and achieved his objectives. His sense of humor readily made friends. He was also a practical joker. One of his favorite pastimes was to go to athletic events and stand by the start line of middle-distance races. As the race started, George would hop over the barrier and run with the runners. He would always keep to the outside so that he did not interfere with the actual race.

The truth was that he was a talented athlete

and would invariably head the race, and about 50 meters from the end he would quickly join the crowd. Normally one would expect that such interference would be prohibited. Still, he would be recognized before the event and thanked for attending and becoming a legend.

George had a very high, IQ and he was always searching for answers to problems. He also realized that his love of fishing was compulsive. He then had arranged with a local retired military colonel to fish in his private lake.

The only rule stipulated was that all fish had to be returned to the lake unharmed. The colonel and George were great friends.

Adjacent to George's favorite spot was a large open sewer. While fishing, he noticed giant rats in the sewer, and he found their movements fascinating. Usually, people would stay away from the population of the sewer.

George had noticed that a stream ran into this sewer, and there were other colonies of rats, but they were all much smaller than in his sewer.

He could not understand why a species of rats

within 100 yards of each other could be so different in size. He then netted one of the smaller rats and put it in the same colony as the more giant rats.

Initially, the smaller rat was isolated, but he grew and was adopted by the larger colony as the weeks passed.

George was fascinated by this development, and he decided that he needed to solve the mystery of different growth patterns. Finally, he came to the logical conclusion: the water in the sewer was far more beneficial to the rats. George decided to take some of the water and feed a few of his pet rabbits and observe the results.

It was no surprise that the rabbits selected became much more significant and healthier than the others. A sample of the water was taken to a chemist for analysis. The only result was that the water was slightly contaminated but not harmful to humans.

George realized that this left the field wide open for further investigation.

During his holiday, she took a part-time job at the local hospital as an assistant to the bakery department. One of his duties was to take tablets to the patients, including those unfortunate souls with terminal illnesses.

In this ward, he knew some of the patients, and he wished that he had the means to cure them.

A flash of brilliance possessed George, and he worried about the ethics involved in his idea. He thought long and hard about his vision. He felt that these people were going to die very soon, and maybe his water could help.

After weeks of indecision, he decided to try and treat three of the terminally ill patients. The three patients were two females and one male. He decided to put a small amount of the 'sewer water' daily in their tea and observe the results. He had decided not to carry on with this exercise if the results were not effective.

The first two weeks showed no improvement, but to the surprise of all the medical staff, there was a dramatic improvement in all three patients by week three.

Total disbelief was an understatement, knowing the history of any UK hospital had three terminally ill patients shown such a reversal of their illness.

It was decided to keep this information secret until the hospital authorities had completed their inquiries. But, fortunately, the three patients continued to progress.

It was complicated to explain to the families that the possible transfer to other wards or other hospitals could be imminent.

However, it was inevitable that an inquiry would follow when the senior medical authorities became aware of the event. George followed the history of the three patients until they were transferred to another hospital. He spoke to the nurses and asked them what had happened to the terminally ill patients who had been shipped out to another hospital.

The nurses could not help with any information.

The local authorities were entirely baffled by the progress of the three patients.

Behind the scenes, many meetings were held. It was decided to evacuate all patients from the original terminally ill ward and modernize and paint it.

In time the three patients continued with their recovery.

They were allowed to return to everyday life with the proviso that they could be recalled at any time.

This incident was only a prelude to a full enquiry by selected experts. The enquiry eventually published a report saying that the only words they could use were miraculous recovery, but the investigation is ongoing.

George realized that he was now 'behind the eight ball.' In other words, he was encountering the biggest dilemma of his life.

George knew that if he made public the true story, he would suffer the most ridicule of all time. But, on the other hand, many seriously ill people could be helped. He needed confidential support, and he needed it urgently.

His father noticed a considerable change in George's attitude to life.

The policy that George's father had adopted was

to allow his son to run his life without interference.

Still, he thought that perhaps it was now time to have a 'heart to heart talk with George. So both George's father and mother spoke with him, and they were careful and kind in their conversation.

Albert Francis was a man of great stature and stood a head above George while telling George that they had noticed a change in his attitude and wondered if they could help.

George's mother, Irma Francis, contrasted with her husband, petite in stature with big blue eyes and full lips. Still, she was, without doubt, the most dominant in their partnership and, without hesitation, joined the conversation by saying, "it is essential for children to trust their parents. A problem shared is a problem halved". George immediately reflected on this comment and thought that he had the best parents in the world. George responded by saying he would reveal his story to understand that they would believe him and keep confidential information. Being a legal professional, George's father responded by saying that "I am a lawyer; my son and all my clients trust me with confidential information."

George relayed his whole story to both his parents, and his father responded by saying, "son your mother and I are immensely proud of you and your news.

For many years people who called Marconi a fake looked ok at the result. Never give up on your dreams'".

Albert said that he thought that although George's experiment was risky, he had been very ethical in his approach. Perhaps it would be worthwhile to get more evidence.

He suggested that George contact the chemist again and get a written report to prove that this water was harmless to humans. The next step would be to contact a patent expert and take out a patent. His father said he would organize the patent and give the product a name.

George's father also committed himself to locating the three patients, talking with them and advising them that he was a lawyer.

Therefore, it would be in their best interests to engage his company in a pro bono agreement.

It was also critical to have a comprehensive chemical analysis of the water.

Naturally, this analysis had to be carried out using the very best chemical analyst experts, and the father would arrange that.

George embraced his parents individually and told them that he loved them with all his heart. The crusade was now a family affair. The family had no idea of what they had unlocked. This story was only just starting.

George realized that they needed more evidence, and it was agreed to select more than three terminally ill patients.

On his rounds in the hospital, George carefully selected six of the terminally ill patients for his treatment. He overheard the nurses mentioning that these patients only had a few days to live.

He was very relaxed because he knew that he was helping and not hindering the patients' progress.

George was confident that the result must be the same, and when the time passed as sure as night follows the day, the results were the same. The hospital authorities were shocked, and the word spread that divine influence was at work.

Initially, some well-meaning Christians arrived at the hospital gates and set up a little grotto for homage.

The police soon removed the grotto, but they could not stop devotees from walking past the hospital and pausing to say a silent prayer. As a result, a new commission was incorporated to carry out further investigations into the latest developments.

Albert had now secretly assumed a leading role and had patented the water and received a comprehensive analysis of the total ingredients of the water.

After the water analysis, he arranged for an expert to reproduce a laboratory sample from known physical ingredients. Unfortunately, it was difficult initially to get a replica.

The only solution was to take the expert to the sewer under the pretext that this was not the actual site. Still, similar conditions existed at the accurate location.

The expert spent many days examining all the various components and the water. Then, through trial and error, he finally created a replica in the laboratory as requested.

The expert had no idea why he had been involved but was thankful for the business.

With this information at hand, Albert felt comfortable presenting the information necessary to produce this extraordinary water.

George's father told him that he must always keep their progress secret.

His exact words to his son were, "remember, Alexander Fleming discovered penicillin by chance and through mere observation. This was the discovery of the century and saved thousands of lives when it was developed."

Then, jokingly, he added, "maybe it is about time that Lourdes water had a competitor."

The scientific society was entirely baffled by 'nearly dead' people who could hope to live. However, they still had no answer to their prayers.

George and his father realized that eventually,

they had to release the information to save countless lives. Still, they did not know how to go about do finally agreed that this was a problem that needed urgent attention. Obviously, because of Albert's experience, he had to take a lead role to overcome this problem.

George's father had many confidential friends in the legal and government section. So he decides to arrange a meeting involving experts in the Secret Services, Police, Law & Order.

He now had the delicate problem of discussing a hypothetical situation with critical, influential, but busy people.

His immediate attention was drawn to Hector Brue of MI.5, who was very reliable. He rang his friend Hector and asked if they could meet somewhere in private. Hector was delighted to connect with his old friend, and they agreed to meet in the lounge of a popular local hotel. When Albert and Hector met face-to-face, they shook hands.

Knowing what Albert preferred, Hector ordered a couple of drinks and took seats in a corner, diagonally across the bar area. They discussed many miscellaneous subjects, and finally, Hector suggested, "I think that we should now talk about the subject of this meeting."

Albert told Hector that he would use fictional characters because real characters have not given him authority to speak on their behalf. Hector agreed.

Albert had a significant dilemma involving his son, George. He wanted some solid advice to put him on the right path.

Continuing, Albert said that he had come across a case that could have worldwide implications.

It was a discovery that was potentially as big as penicillin. He realized that he would have to create fictitious events and people to explain.

Hector, a straightforward individual, said, "Let's cut out the crap and call a spade a spade." Albert hesitated and then said he had a friend who had discovered a cure for some terminal illnesses.

Albert said that the 'treatment' was administered to nine critically ill humans and proved successful. Although this is news, it needed to be kept under wraps until they knew how and when to use it. He explained that they see the problem they would have with big pharmaceutical companies but was excited about the possibility of curing the terminally ill.

Albert continued by saying, "What we need to know is the best way forward so that we can operate and administer the cure?"

Hector sat in silence for a few minutes and then said, "You have given me a conundrum, and I will need some time to get back to you with a practical answer."

"I am grateful for meeting me at short notice and know that you have the biggest network of friends and professional colleagues, and I look forward to your reply," concluded Albert.

When Albert returned home, he told George that there was no guarantee but that he had set the wheels in motion to sort out a plan of action.

He also advised George to stay away from the sewer until they had devised a concrete plan of action.

Hector eventually rang back approximately three weeks later they agreed to meet at the venue of their previous meeting. At the meeting, Harold explained the situation to date.

He had met with a select body of government, police, MI5, medical experts.

Hector did a great job of outlining a possible dilemma, and the result of the meeting was unanimous to actions, which had to satisfy the following three conditions:

a) 100% secure health conditions

b) introduction under total security

c) introduction into the market as a "right to try" for terminal people only.

The committee volunteered to select a place and time for the highly confidential trial, named Z69, to be carried out. A destination for this exercise was to be carried out in a small local hospital, and a dozen 'right to try' patients were selected.

The patients selected were all in proximity to the hospital, thus allowing visitors to attend as usual. It was the first time that any UK patient had the option under the law for treatment through a 'right to try' option.

The hospital staff was told that this operation was strictly confidential. They were mandated to sign a legal document under the Official Secrets Act.

The patients were briefed and reminded that the treatment they were about to undergo was new. Still, the preliminary results of a similar but informal trial had encouraging signs.

Unfortunately, two patients died before receiving any treatment. Meaning that only ten terminally ill patients could receive their first dose of 'the cure.'

However, all the patients were closely monitored by the hour, and the medical staff captured statistical information.

This information was immediately sent to all the parties involved in this highly confidential trial.

The weeks passed quickly, and the first signs of improvement were in week three, as expected. The visitors who witnessed this improvement were very emotional, but they were advised to remain calm. At the end of six weeks, all ten had improved immensely. However, the patients were kept in hospital for a further period to monitor and ensure no repercussions.

Eventually, after six months, all the patients were allowed to return home. Still, daily visits continued to be carried out in every case. Everyone involved in the highly confidential trial Z69 realized an event of such importance could not be kept secret forever. Finally, permission was given to the patent holder of this new drug to produce supplies under a license.

Albert Francis and his son George were joint holders of this license. They joined forces with a pharmaceutical manufacturing organization to produce the new product in bulk.

After considerable time Albert and George agreed to name their product 'VITaLIFE'.

However, they realized that the name was only temporary since it would have to be approved and conform to strict rules and regulations.

Through further research trials, they could claim that a terminal illness involving potential terminal growth showed positive results in a patient that used VITaLIFE.

Still, they both understood that due to the cost involved for further research and development, many illnesses VITaLIFE could not cure.

Years of use of VITaLIFE eventually allowed it to become a household name. The life of the 'Francis' family changed beyond all recognition.

George was no longer a teenager, and his father had become a businessman instead. Hence, as a result, the lawyer. The family became wealthy, but this did not change George, who played pranks at athletic events.

One onlooker, who watched George having fun at the various athletic meetings, recognized that he was a serious athlete and decided to interview him.

When George had finished one of his fun runs, he managed to intercept and interview him. Ho asked George whether he was afraid of being beaten in a race and never formally competed in the athletic events.

George was quite surprised by the question and did his best to dodge the answer and was surprised to learn that the man he was talking to was a coach for the British Olympic team.

But, George said, "I have never given it a thought because I enjoy the notoriety of being Wilson."

"Who is Wilson," asked the coach.

George replied, "My father used to read a comic, and one of the stars was a chap named Wilson who would go to the main events and do what I do now.

So, I simply thought it would be fun to run and entertain people during the severe events." "I am amazed! Do you not realize that maybe you are better than the other runners?" replied the coach.

George agreed to meet up with the coach and join him at a local athletics club for some formal training.

The coach asked him what his favorite race was, and George replied, "Any distance between 1000 meters to 5000 meters".

The coach had arranged for several runners and George to run over a 1000 meters race on the ground. He told George that he wanted him to run the fastest race but forget about his competitors.

The race became an absolute farce. George had a lead over 50 meters and won in a canter. When the coach looked at his stopwatch, he realized that George was only seconded outside the British record. The coach was speechless that he had found a natural athlete who was not vitally interested in running.

The coach spoke to George, who was completely relaxed, and he excitedly asked, "George, my old potato, do you just realize what you have just done?"

George replied, "I could probably have done better if I had tried harder."

The coach responded by saying, "You are only seconds outside the British record, and I am not letting you leave this club until you promise me that you will let me be your coach and you will take running seriously."

George promised with one proviso. "Ok, what is it?"

"I have a very responsible business opportunity which is taking up a lot of my time, and it is more important to me than anything else," was George's reply.

"If I can make you better than Wilson, will that be enough to give me six hours a week?" asked the coach.

George, with his brilliant sense of humor, realized

that this man, who at this time had not mentioned his name was superior in the fun game and was to become his best friend.

"I will give you six hours a week if you tell me your name," agreed George.

"I am James Little, the Head coach to Olympic Team."

George organized his time to contribute to the advance of the VITaLIFE program and his new friend, coach James. The progress of the newly named VITaLIFE project was meteoric, and his father had organized various outsources to cope with the demand. After several years George and his father had sold out VITaLIFE to a multinational company that had the resources to handle the project. George kept his promise to spend six hours a week improving his fitness and technique.

He held British records in races from 1000 to 5000 without ever losing interest in VITaLIFE.

The company with the license to run VITaLIFE went from strength to strength.

The discovery of this medical revolution had to be recognized and received worldwide acclaim.

Therefore, it further decided that the original award winner should be George Francis, and he received an M.B.E. In addition, George was recognized as the youngest winner of an M.B.E. award.

The years ahead were very kind to George. He married his wife Susan, and they had three children, and they lived in a large house in the Midlands.

George never forgot his love of the unseen mysteries around us. He set up scholarships for suitable students who had this unending curiosity like him. He also became very interested in athletics and football.

He became a committee member of several athletic clubs and an avid supporter of Manchester City FC. George never missed a game at home or away and planned his personal and work life around the Manchester City FC schedule.

Upon reflection of his life, George wondered why he had earned such underserving recognition and honors in his life.

Everyone else could have told George that he belonged to that elite circle that needed to be classed as a genius at birth.

THE END

THE SOUL MASTER

George Hobart Stevens was a man with many talents and blessed with more than his share of good fortune, but his crude and wicked temper ultimately flawed him. His sarcastic wit disarmed opponents with little effort. His talents enabled him to achieve fame and fortune in a short time. During his teenage years, he achieved stardom on whatever stage he performed.

His prowess on the sports field could only be described as superb. He was a most talented actor, and his female conquests were legendary.

George's childhood was typical of his generation. His parents were classified as working class.

His education had been gained through sheer hard work in a very competitive system where only the most innovative youngsters could progress by proving their credentials and having the luck to win a scholarship. Early childhood would be difficult, but George was learning most of life's essential skills.

He would often relate a story of his early years when he played outdoors with his pals. The games that they played would typically include a ball.

On occasions, they would play with bicycle tires.

He told the story of one of his pals who would arrive with a car tire and the envy that he experienced when he had only a battered bicycle tire. This simple incident made him determined to succeed at all costs.

George never possessed a car tire, but subconsciously, the scruffy kid with the beautiful black tire sparked the drive to outdo all his playmates.

If ever an ambition was spawned, then those early underdog years that George suffered would prove to be the most valuable.

George's talents quickly isolated him as a man amongst men and a future leader. His rapid climb up the commercial ladder was assured, and now at the age of forty years, he awaited his call to greatness with calm.

He knew that he was due to be appointed as the youngest Chief Executive ever of 'multi-Plastics,' which is a multi-national company, possibly within the next five days. George had finished his latest assignment and knew that he should not embark on an immediate project.

The summer season was in full flow. He had become bored by the isolation he was enduring in his palatial office.

The bright sunshine was too much of a temptation to remain indoors, so George decided that he should leave the office early and drive over to the Lillisham Golf Club, where he intended to have a relaxing afternoon doing nothing.

On entering the club lounge, George quickly perched himself on one of the high bar stools. "Your usual Sir," asked the barman. "Yes, you should know," was the reply. George idly scanned the room for some intellectually compatible company, to whom he wished to entertain with his versatile and sparkling conversation.

Old Arthur was sitting by the window talking to Bernard. Still, he thought that perhaps their conversation would be complicated going.

Apart from one or two other no-hopers, the room was relatively empty. George knew that he could not demean himself by talking the daily nonsense of golf swing techniques to the club's professional or some other topic.

His mind was somewhere in "no man's" land as he savored his favorite drink of Napoleon Brandy. During his second sip of the drink, he became acutely aware that an invisible force was slowly pulling him from his stool. The momentary sensation was not alarming to him, but his subconscious told him that the force was irresistible.

George did not realize, but in that instant, his earthly life was ending abruptly.

The stool leaned for a brief instant at an alarming angle before the almighty clatter and thud informed the few onlookers that the man sitting at the end of the bar had come against the forces of nature and had most positively lost.

Paddy Lynch, one of the club's groundsmen, said to his pal Freddy Hughes, "Jesus, did you see that

Fred, the big guy at the end of the bar, has just fallen off his stool? He must have drunk more than he could handle".

Getting up from their seats, they picked up George from his prone position. They immediately realized that he was far from being drunk and seriously unwell.

One of the "apostolic trains" was ready for its daily journey to its celestial destination. The duty Soul Master was expecting George Stevens on the afternoon's train. The train is invisible to the human eye. It is structured so that the souls with the best merit ratings would be put in the first carriage(s), and subsequent carriages would be allocated according to merit ratings.

The relative comfort or discomfort of the carriage had remained the same throughout history. How a unit of transport could accommodate such opposing values was the work of the ultimate genius.

George had arrived on this pre-destined date to inherit his just rewards. The Soul Master who met George on his arrival explained to him some brief facts about his future.

He explained that every arrival would have a rating. This rating could be improved while in his celestial home, or he could be sent back to earth and given another chance to improve his performance.

Many millions had served other earthly time and returned with much better ratings. It was not unusual for a soul to be returned many times before obtaining its ultimate rating. When a soul was returned to earth, they were born anew and did not always know of their previous existence. This information was very confusing to George, but he was afraid to ask any questions.

The Soul Master explained that his role would be to make every effort to assist all the souls under his control. Finally, the Soul Master gave George a brief view of his future potential eternal home.

Even though this view, was short it was sufficient for George to realize that he must do everything within his capabilities to return.

Although, of course, George did not like the overriding aspect, he knew that he had to come to terms with it, was that he was a nobody.

With the structure of his new soul being transparent to everyone, he realized that he would need help to lower his high rating.

When his interview finished, he returned to the point allocated to him.

He was conscious of his new surroundings. His rating was significantly higher than most, and the relative indifference to his plight hurt him enormously. The thought uppermost in George's mind was how can I improve my rating freely with the common herd. It was ironic that this particular thought was the one that had never entered his mind during his life on earth. However hard he tried, he could not hide his sinful ratings. He realized that if he persisted in these efforts, he could incur higher ratings.

Within a short period, George knew that the only way to mitigate his shame was to follow the instructions of his Soul Master and start by achieving total humility.

The Soul Master told George that he had examined his rating and had decided to return him to earth because this was by far the best way to improve his rating. So, George was returned to the world. Back on earth, the ambulance had been called, and Paddy Lynch and Freddy Hughes were following instructions on the method of artificial resuscitation.

The ambulance arrived within minutes, and the paramedics took over. George did not respond immediately, and the medics were on the verge of stopping the treatment when a sudden response was noticed. On arrival at the hospital, he was immediately rushed into the Accident and Emergency Unit. He underwent all the necessary tests before being discharged into a General Ward. One of the leading doctors said, "I can't understand how George appears to be making an unbelievable recovery" The time that George spent convalescing was the happiest time of his life.

He knew that he had a future in the "after-life and this enormous responsibility was placed upon him. His wife and three children visited regularly, but George never mentioned his time with the Soul Master.

He was aware that he had a mission to fulfill, but he would need time to complete it.

He realized that he had a message to give to the

world. But unfortunately, he would have many opponents waiting to ridicule him as another bogus missionary trying to fool an unsuspecting public.

Despite his thoughts on the future, he knew for sure that he had truth on his side, and he had been handed a golden opportunity to become a true disciple.

George was eventually discharged from the hospital three weeks later. The cause of his problem was diagnosed as a temporary shock to the heart caused by the fall.

During his time in hospital, he reflected on his "near-death" experience. He realized that he would now have to conduct his life differently.

He had plenty of time to consider his current position. He thought that he must be the luckiest man alive. How many humans get the chance to see their future celestial paradise and know with absolute certainty that there was a "life after death"

His happiness in the hospital was overwhelming. His visitors could see that he was a much better human than before his accident.

The wise words given to him by his Soul Master would be followed in all circumstances.

George was discharged from the hospital, and two weeks later, he returned to work as Chief Executive of multi-Plastics.

Everyone who knew George soon realized that he was a completely different person, and the change was incredible. Gone was the arrogant attitude to be replaced by a much calmer understanding approach.

He made it his business to visit the factory frequently and talk with the workers.

During his visits, he would uncover many of the workers' worries and apply solutions immediately. As a result, the word spread throughout the business that a man was respected and admired. In a recent visit, he had spoken with one of the workers about his son, who was discharged from the marines because of an injury caused in battle.

Unfortunately, his son was unable to get his injury attended to because of the prohibitive cost involved.

George called his company doctor and instructed him to get the full details and recommendations regarding this case.

The doctor reported back with the type of injury and the cost of treatment.

The treatment would have to be carried out in the U.S.A.

When George received the information, he called the company doctor. He asked him to arrange for the treatment to be carried out. He also asked the doctor to keep the matter confidential because this was a private agreement between the worker and himself.

The ex-marine was treated in the USA and fully recovered, and George paid all costs. Sometimes personal stories are so secret that it is impossible to keep them under wraps.

Within a week, the whole factory knew of this case. A segment of the workers arranged for the soldier to come to the factory to meet the man who had solved his problem and given him his life back. They also arranged for an audience to be in attendance when the soldier and his father met George.

The meeting was very emotional, particularly for the father, who had witnessed a real man looking after his fellow man.

There were many instances involving George, which he kept secret.

Two years passed before George realized that his real mission in life was to talk to the world about our celestial destiny and the meaning of the word truth.

One of the many friends that George had made was a Baptist minister. He decided to contact him and ask permission to give a presentation on religion in general.

The minister agreed to arrange the script. Arriving at the chapel adjacent to the church, George was met by his friend, the minister.

The minister explained that he had told the congregation that he would forego his sermon and invite George to give his presentation instead. George stood in the pulpit and introduced himself. He said that his name was George Stevens, and he was the current CEO of Multi-Plastics. George was amazed at the beautiful church and the large congregation.

In a lighter vein, George said this was the first time he had stood in a pulpit, and he felt a little like Mussolini but without the hat. He assured the congregation that he would not be giving a long sermon n and take any questions at the end.

George felt true happiness and introduced his subject with 'TRUTH.' This word was associated with many similar words. Still, the most common would be 'HONESTY.' He assured his audience that every word of his submission would be accurate.

George said that a few years had passed since he had suffered a near-death experience.

He said that he knew that the phrase 'near-death experience' was a big turn-off for many people. However, he had to admit that he was also very skeptical before he experienced it.

He also stated that some individuals may tell lies and just want fame or notoriety. George explained that he was at a golf club when some invisible force pulled him, and he fell to the floor.

His soul was immediately transported to a heavenly place where he met his Soul Master. The latter explained that this would be the place for his final and eternal rest. He also confirmed that many souls who arrived with bad ratings could be sent back to earth to resume their earthly life and substantially improve their ratings.

The feeling of peace was indescribable, and it was his dearest wish to stay there.

George paused for a second. Then, he resumed and explained that this meeting was the high point of his entire life. He said to the congregation, "The first word that I commenced my talk with was TRUTH (The truth sets you free.) I would ask you to explain why I should tell you lies; I can't find words to convince you, and I understand that.

Maybe when you get to know me better, you will find the joy of believing the truth", continuing; he said that the Soul Master had explained to him that it had been decided, because of his high rating, to return him to earth and regain his earthly body and thus give him a second chance to arrive later with a much better rating.

At this stage of his speech, he felt that the spirit was helping him with his words. He then returned to his opening word, and that was the word truth. He knew without any debate that truth was the one word that we all understand, but it is the most difficult to use in practice.

George said that he would continue with his speech but paused for a short time so that the audience realized that he had spoken every word of truth. At that moment, a man in the congregation said, "I think that your message is good, and I would give my wife's right hand to believe you" (mild laughter from the audience.)

George replied by saying I hear daily, in ordinary conversation, people saying, "you would not know the truth if you saw it with your own eyes," this is unfortunately true.

It is also true to say that some people will tell lies because the truth is inconvenient.

My answer to you is "seek, and you will find. Before I met with my Soul Master, I would say that I belonged to a group of disbelievers. I thought it was rubbish to believe in an afterlife, but I have seen evidence of the afterlife, and I know you will consider that I am telling you the truth in time. George said he would change the rest of his presentation and go straight to questions.

The first question was from a little old lady who asked, "why is the afterlife so secret?

The response was that God, in His wisdom, had

decided that trust was also a valuable asset to people in their quest for redemption.

There were many more exciting questions, and George did his best to answer all of them. George said that he had much more information to pass on to the congregation at the end of question time.

He would return, if invited, to clarify his experience with his Soul Master. The Baptist Minister said "that he would canvas his followers and let George know of the outcome.

It was purely coincidental that television had many channels, particularly YouTube, about life and death experiences and the afterlife and professional experts speaking about controlling one's life by being better than good and always telling the truth. Yet, despite all this attention, people are still very skeptical and treat the matter very carefully.

The Baptist minister informed George that the church hall was available for his following speech two weeks later. He also added that more people would be in attendance.

George arrived at the chapel and was pleasantly surprised when people stood outside the church because all the seats had been taken indoors. George climbed the two stairs to the pulpit and greeted his audience, "Good morning to everyone who has ventured out on this cold morning." He said, "I am very flattered with the gathering and wished to talk in more detail about the celestial home that I had visited. I wish to acknowledge that maybe several people would think that they were listening to a fairy tale."

He recounted that he collapsed at the golf club, and he next recalled meeting with his Soul Master. He further stressed that many such accounts given by other life or death recollections could be traced to mental or drug or operations or identity problems.

Still, He assured the congregation that he had none of these ailments.

 When he met his Soul Master, he realized that he was in the company of a beautiful, calm spirit. He was shown to the place that George should aspire to and given time to observe and encounter the feeling of inner peace. To attempt to describe this sensational meeting is impossible.

However, suppose you can recollect some of the memories you hold dear and multiply that feeling by hundreds of times. In that case, you may come close to my experience.

From my prior statements, you may understand that I am fearless with every word that I use.

What is more incredible is that I know my goals in life and the possible rewards we all can attain.

You can think of thousands of questions, but I can assure you that if you try hard, you may surprise yourself. My last comment reminds me of a song that Marty Robbins sang, "Lord, you gave me a mountain to climb," which finishes with "a mountain that I may never climb, and that is the position some of you may feel that you are experiencing.

The easiest way I can explain my meeting is by using an example. Imagine that you are invited to Buckingham Palace and given a tour of part of the palace. You will come away feeling very honored and tell all your friends.

I have been given a second chance to save my soul and realize that my mountain is very high, but I hope to climb it finally.

I have many plans to achieve, and I can assure each one of you that I will not fail for lack of trying.

Thank you all for coming, I will never desert you, and I look forward to our next meeting".

George returned to his job as CEO of Multi-Plastics and carried out his regular duties. He was always thinking ahead about what he could do to improve the lot of the workforce. He called a meeting of the Board of Directors and reviewed the progress to date.

The situation at the company was satisfactory, and a walk down to the shop floor was necessary.

George was well-liked by the workforce. He would ask various workers what they would do to improve working conditions and working hours to family life.

Some workers thought that the management could improve working conditions, and George made notes of their statements.

On return to the Board Room, George said that he

had a new idea, and he would like to get a general opinion from his colleagues.

He thought that a team consisting of Management and workers would be a feasible idea and, in some respects, a perfect one. So he asked the personnel director to talk with the workers' representatives and organize a separate committee to cover workers' welfare.

The committee was formed and started to produce good results. The workforce realized that they had a true friend at the head of the Board.

 George had always kept his private life out of the spotlight. Still, he knew that now he had a crusade and needed to devote his whole life in the hope that one day he would again meet up with his Soul Master and earn his just rewards.

He realized that he was becoming a local celebrity, and he had now got a huge following.

He arranged through the local authorities to speak to the public.

On the meeting day, he had no nerves because he was confident that his honesty and truth would shine through. Reaching the stage, he noticed that there were several cameras, and his speech was being recorded. He welcomed his audience and said, "It is evident that my previous statements are bearing fruit, and I am sure that there a lot of you who have come to see this extraordinary man who reckons that he has met a Soul Master and knows his future in paradise.

I would clarify this by saying that I hope that I know my future but realize that I have a lot of work to earn my future". He briefly explained his encounter with his Soul Master and the meaning of the truth and faith of the word. Then, he paused for a moment, realizing that his audience was utterly silent and under his control.

Explaining the reason for his pause, he reached out to his audience, explaining that he wished that he knew how to convert every doubter about his honesty.

"It is said that you should never criticize a man before you had walked a few miles in his shoes, so that is probably my message for today.

I have met my Soul, Master and I speak the truth, and I want you to imagine that you have walked a few miles in my shoes. Suppose you can imagine that we have changed places and I was in the audience, and you had met your Soul Master, what a great joy you would experience. I will now tell you about meeting my Soul Master. Some of you have already heard this story, but I will repeat it".

George spent time explaining his encounter with his Soul Master. He spent a lot more time than usual talking in greater detail about the feeling of happiness that he experienced just being in the presence of his Soul Master. He noticed one or two women visibly crying while he was speaking.

Little did he realize that he was fast becoming one of the most charismatic orators in the country.

He explained that his mission was to encounter as many people as possible, either single or in groups or presentations to the public in general. He said he could be contacted by his email, and he gave them his address.

His final words were, "thanks for coming. I leave you with one word TRUTH; it sets you free". George was amazed at the number of emails that he received. He analyzed them and put them into categories. By this method, he responded to the bulk by using one email, and the remainder he attempted to contact them individually.

Later the following week, while at work, he was approached by a local television company and invited to come in to make a recording that eventually would be sold country-wide.

At the same time, various agnostics or Atheists would challenge him to debate and take a lie detector test. He readily agreed, to note that it would be impossible to meet everyone individually.

George spent a lot of his free time speaking with various doubters, and he endured numerous lie detector tests.

He left several of the doubters confused, but he recognized that there was a number unconvinced. As the months and years passed by, George continued his excellent work until late one summer evening. He was not feeling well, and the ambulance was called to take him to the hospital.He was informed that he had pneumonia and he would be detained in the hospital for further treatment.

One evening George was slumbering when he thought that he was meeting with his Soul Master. Instead, he awoke to reality and met his Soul Master, who transported him to his eternal reward.

THE END

CHARLIE BROWNE

Charlie Browne was born in a village on the outskirts of Wigan in Lancashire in the year 1898. He was the only son of William and Margaret Brown. His father was a collier [sic}, and his mother worked in a cotton mill. The father traveled to work on his bicycle every day, and his mother could walk to the mill.

This was the age of the invention of the steam engine, and factories were increasing in the north. In addition, improvements in gaslighting and sewers and the arrival of the first cars revolutionized society. However, still, children were being sent up chimneys to clear blockages and eleven years of age was quite normal for children to go down the coal mines.

Charlie was sent down to the mines by his father, and he was made to work hard. He achieved fame by being the most productive miner in the area, and in his teens, his notoriety was well known.

Reaching the age of 16, he volunteered for the Northern regiment of the British Army.

He, like many of his pals, thought that the army would provide adventure, and the poster 'Your country needs you" was compelling.

He served in England, but eventually, he was sent abroad with thousands of others, including men and boys from Australia, India or New Zealand, and other parts of the commonwealth.

On the 25th of April 1915, Charlie was experiencing the horror of war in a rowing boat attempting to land on the Gallipoli Peninsula.

A reporter commented that shrapnel was taking a heavy toll on the allied troops as they attempted a landing at Cape Hellas. Bodies littered the beaches. It took two days before the allied troops secured the beach area.

Heavy fighting ensued, and by the end of the war, the allies had lost 44000 men while the Ottoman empire lost 87000 men. Charlie experienced the full horrors of war.

He often spoke about how the bodies were buried, and he would comment on the time that the whistle would be blown.

They had to climb out of the trenches and see his mates shot dead as they ran to attack the enemy hand-to-hand combat.

Eventually, when Charlie returned home and settled into civilian life, his grandchildren would persuade him to talk about the war. He had many stories to tell one of the most interesting was when he was on sentry duty in Gallipoli.

Apparently, on this night, the visibility was almost zero. He heard a noise coming from a white shape some thirty yards away.

He challenged the shape with "Halt who goes there" with no effect, he repeated the challenge, and the figure remained silent. Finally, he had no compunction and fired several rounds into the apparent enemy.

On daybreak, he went over to inspect the results of his work only to find that he had shot and killed the regimental mascot goat.

Another good story was when he was employed as a sniper in charge of a local railway line. He was hiding in the lower branches of a tree when a German soldier appeared and sat down to eat his lunch. Charlie had him clearly in his rifle sights, watching him eat his lunch. When the German soldier had finished, he brushed the crumbs off his uniform and returned and walked away. Charlie said it was a beautiful summer day, and he could not possibly shoot the enemy soldier.

He had many stories, some of which he should not be telling his grandchildren. He would often repeat the story that the biggest myth about the war was that the British Army never retreated in disorder. He responded that on occasions, they would run like hell to get away from the enemy.

Two years after returning to civilian life, Charlie married a lovely beauty in 1920 named Margaret. Charlie was a man amongst men, but he was always subservient to Margaret. They had one child, and they called him Richard.

He was born on the 1st of July 1921; he was sent down to the mines like his father.

At 12 years, he attended school until his father decided that it was time to earn his keep. So, Richard joined his father in the mines, and they worked as a team.

Charlie was now in his mid-thirties, and he expected his son to work as hard as he did.

There was always competition between the miners regarding the number of tubs that they could fill. Invariably Charlie would always win.

The social life of the mining community usually revolved around the local public house, and the place for the women was in the house, so outdoor events became men only.

The main events that occupied the miners' free time were drinking, horse racing, bare-knuckle fights, bowls, football, and cockfighting Charlie became the senior male in his village and controlled many of the events.

He was particularly keen on organizing the miners, particularly about absenteeism. He was usually the first man on his shift and managed the workforce.

He was one of the village's first residents to buy his own house, and he was always proud to boast about this. His time in the forces was to change him drastically. He rose to the rank of sergeant, but he never bullied his men.

The boys who had volunteered to fight for King and Country and had gone on an exciting mission were soon to experience what can only be described as a mission to hell.

The experience of seeing their countrymen slaughtered would change them forever. The statement that the recruits went to war as men and came home as heroes were not entirely true.

In many cases, the men came home as wrecks. Charlie returned to civilian life and returned to the mines; he was appointed to chargehand. He started work and was soon into the routine every day.

He would allow the workforce time to take a break for refreshments.

Upon returning to work after the holidays, the heavy mining machinery slowly moved in and out of the coal face. At the same time, the men sat in a small alcove, partially closed by a 'brattice' cloth. They were enjoying their only meal break of the shift.

Their 'snap-tins were opened, and ribald opening comments had been made. The dialogue was simple, and the camaraderie was obvious.

Two men were arguing about "who owns Malta" when the argument was getting rather heated; one wit said, "I don't know, but Jack Jarvis {race-horse trainer} trained it" This caused colossal laughter and killed the argument.

"Now then," said Charlie Froust, "What do you do when you get a ring-tailed monkey sitting beside of you in the pub" Bennie Dean responded first, "Well Charlie" I suppose you must either give him a banana or a kick up the arse" and send him on his way. "Why, Charlie, what are you trying to tell us," Asked Bennie.

"Well," said Charlie, "I went up to the Labour club last night, and I was sat at the bar having a pint with old Dick Brow. He was telling me about a neighbor of his who had won first prize on the treble chance. He said that two workmen were servicing his car in his garage, and one said to the other that he was going to put a bet on Littlewoods". The owner of the house asked the workman, "Will you place a bet on me?"

"Yes, give me your numbers."

Littlewoods scribbled down ten numbers and wrote down the simple perm and handed him the paper.

Any eight from ten and he won, and he had nine lines of treble chance correct. Charlie said that is fantastic and asked, "How much of a gift and he give to the guy placing the bet?"

"Nothing," said Littlewoods.

Charlie said, "There is nothing as queer as folk."

Charlie said that he had finished his conversation with Dick Brown when two men came into the club and sat next to him.

"I minded my own business when one of these fellows came behind me and landed me with a hard punch, I shot off my stool, and I lay on the floor for a minute. When I got up, the fellow was looking at me, and he said, I am very sorry, but I have hit the wrong chap. I took one look at him, and I said, no, you have not, you have hit the right chap, and I set into him, and I gave him a real good hammering".

"I heard about that," said little Billy McGinty. "I believe that there was blood everywhere".

"Now you are talking," said Charlie.

"I got stuck into him, and I knocked him across the tables. I picked him up and asked him whether he had had enough, the blood was covering his face, and he was unable to speak, so I let him be."

"What happened to his mate?" asked one of the miners.

"Mate, he was no mate; when I challenged him, he buggered off like a rat up a drainpipe," replied

Charlie.

"Bloody hell Charlie," said little Cyril McGloin, "it's a wonder you didn't kill him!"

"It's not the first time it has happened to me," said Charlie. "I am getting quite a name and becoming a local celebrity. It was only the other day that I was approached by the Freemasons to join them and help them to cope with those Irish navies up at Green Lane."

"Right time up," shouted the Foreman, "let's get back to work."

The men shuffled off to the coalface, and the shift continued. Charlies' actual title was underground deputy. Each miner had a tally.

A metal disc was handed to the deputy as they boarded the lift to go underground and was returned to the miner when he left the lift.

If the deputy had any disks left by any chance, there would be an immediate inquiry. It was infrequent that the deputy had any disks, but it did happen several times to Charlie. Immediately all miners were not allowed to leave the premises until a solution had been achieved.

On one occasion, a miner had been trapped in a collapse of coal.

On the other occasion, there was a fatality involving a miner being run over by one of the fully laden tubs.

It was not unusual to have rock falls while the miners were putting up the wooden roof supports. On one occasion, Charlie was involved, and all his colleagues left the scene. He was trapped for hours before anyone dared to return.

Finally, when Charlie had finished his shift and accounted for all his men, he returned home.

 Later that evening, Charlie had his bath in the large bathtub in front of the fire, while his wife Margaret was putting his rabbit stew on the table, there was a loud knock on the front door informing them both that an unwelcome visitor was about to shatter the peace of the household.

Margaret went to the door and was faced by two uniformed policemen, "Is Charlie in?" said the policeman with the three-striped uniform.

"Why do you want to know?" asked Margaret. With that remark, the two policemen brushed Margaret aside and entered the house.

Charlie, by this time, was about three fields away, having escaped through the back door.

He was having a bath in a large metal tub, and

he grabbed his clothes and fled through the back door. When he had jumped over the garden fence, he dropped his woolen jumper, but he had no time to return and try to reclaim it.

Having searched the house, the Sergeant said, "Tell Charlie when he comes home that we need to talk to him about a fight in the pub the other night. The fellow that he was fighting with is in a serious condition in the hospital. The Doctors are not sure whether he will live or die. We need to put Charlie in the cells for his good. There is more than a few who would like to bang Charlie about."

"Right," responded Margaret. "When he comes home, I will tell him".

So, Charlie lay doggo for a few hours and slowly made his way home by the route that only he knew.

It was a cold night, and he was frozen stiff "Where have you been?" asked Margaret

"Been?" said Charlie sarcastically, "where do you think I have been?"

"You certainly haven't been to London to see the Queen," said Margaret.

"Why am I in trouble?" asked Charlie.

"Well, the police think that that you have possibly killed a chap in the pub the other night."

"Bloody hell," wailed Charlie, "is the bastard about to cock his clogs." "Charlie, this is no laughing matter. You had better come back when the coast is clear".

Margaret had hardly uttered these words when they were both conscious of the noise outside of the house.

Several of the mates of the man in the hospital were shouting for Charlie to come out.

"Margaret, hand me my coat and give me a few bottles of ale to put in the pockets."

Charles went through the front door swinging his coat around like a gaucho about to rope a steer. None of the men could get near to Charlie because of the flying beer bottles. In truth, none of the men wanted to get near Charlie because of his fierce reputation.

Charlie was in hiding for many weeks, and he did not return home. His wife Margaret did not know where he was, and indeed his employer missed his influence at the coal face. Luckily for Charlie, the severely beaten man made a full recovery and resumed his role in society.

When Charlie came home, he was more or less pleased that the charge against him of grievously bodily harm was the only one pressed by the police. He was arrested and placed in a prison cell. On the court day, things were going Charlie's way, the authority having no witnesses and relying on circumstantial evidence.

Charlie had not been trained in the art of verbal survival, and he was to make the one fatal mistake that would earn him a prison sentence.

It was on the second day of the proceedings when the plaintiff stood up to give his account of the beating that he had received at the hands of Charlie.

"Will you recount in your own words and in your own time the happenings of the day of the assault?" Asked the magistrate.

"Well, your honor, I was sitting having a quiet print at the Labour club when Charlie stood up and gave me a clout round the ear."

Charlie listening to this appeared to remain calm, but as the plaintiff went on and poured out more lies, it was all too much for Charlie. Charlie jumped up. His face was as red as a peacock, "You are a lying bastard he shouted."

"Quiet in court," snapped the magistrate. Charlie would not be silenced; his temper was now his master. "When you get outside of this court, I will give you some more."

As soon as he uttered those fatal words, "I will give you some more," the magistrate banged his gravel on the block of wood and said, "There is little point in going on with these proceedings I find Charles Froust guilty by his admission of the crime of which he stands accused. He will serve a sentence of two months in jail". "Bugger me," said Charlie, addressing the magistrate, you are as big an upstart as that bastard over there."

The case concluded by the magistrate saying, "and an additional one month for contempt of court."

Charlie had lost, game, set, and match. Charlie served his time and was now regarded as the hard man of the village.

He would become involved in what was later called "prize-fighting" but was commonly known as "catch as catch can."

This method of fighting involved all kinds of combat, from grappling to kicking and punching.

Onlookers would travel many miles to see the locals engaging in fist and wrestling fights. Charlie took on all comers and was never beaten.

He often took a beating but would eventually prove the winner through what was referred to as 'Charlie's Hammer.'

The fight would only end when one of the participants could not get up from the floor. All the local onlookers knew that Charlie had a Liverpool idol named Kid Tanner, the original joker.

Tanner, who was eventually world champion, would pretend to be taking a beating and wink at his trainers in his corner. Then when the time was right, Tanner would eliminate his opponent with ease. The crowd never knew, but Charlie had laid all kinds of bets, including naming the round. The new onlooker would see Charlie taking what looked like a severe beating. They would see Charlie's opponent laughing to the crowd, often commenting, "Is this the hard man that I have come to lick?"

Inevitably, when the chosen round was called, Charlie would deliver his hammer blow. He did not care where he landed it. Still, the locals knew when it was coming, Charlie would shout, "Here comes Pretty Polly," and the punch often traveling no more than six inches was powerful enough to dent an iron door. It was not uncommon to hear the opponents' ribs crack. The drama was intense. The locals loved it. Charlie Froust was the undisputed champion of the world, as far as they were concerned. The many stories of Charlie's powers followed him into later life.

He was very much a man in demand. He was recruited by several organizations such as the Freemasons, an organization with a vendetta against Catholics. He would be invited to oversee their events and ensure that there was no trouble.

As part of his recreational activities, he would snare rabbits and always had at least a dozen chickens.

Charlies' lifestyle suited him, and he was very rarely upset with others outside of the family. Margaret had no difficulty in organizing him daily. She was a typical mother and grandmother.

The grandchildren thought the world of her, and they usually were afraid of their grandfather. However, there was one memorable instant when the grandchildren had been invited to dinner. Grandson Richard was struggling to cut a piece of bacon. Richard strained with everyone watching him, only to see the bacon fly off his plate onto the floor. Grandfather jumped from his chair, picked up the bacon piece, and immediately scolded Richard about his table manners. There was a deathly hush until Margaret interfered and consoled Richard by saying to Charlie, "that could happen to any one of us " Margaret's daughter-in-law Josephine was always a notable absentee from any family occasions involving Charlie. He was very scathing about Josephine having five children. Josephine had grandparents who were Irish, and that was a big problem with Charlie. Later in life, Charlie decided to retire from daily work in the coal mines.

He suffered an injury down the mine and was awarded a lump sum in compensation, which would be sufficient income before he received his pension. Margaret always encouraged Charlie to spend his spare time outside, which was ideal for Charlie. However, there were occasions when Charlie did not come home at night. Margaret knew that he was probably snaring some form of wildlife. He would capture a Linett which is, a small songbird of the finch family. This bird was noted for its song. Charlie would catch one and bring it home and put it in a cage. Once the bird was regularly fed, they would start to sing, and it had a remarkable repertoire. Charlie had a love for all wildlife, and after a few months, he would release the linnet back into the wild and capture a replacement.

Probably the hobby that Charlie most enjoyed was green crown bowls. He would on occasions visit New Brighton, a town on the Cheshire side of the Mersey River.

There was a particular bowling green where the rich and famous visited. Charlie would go onto the green when he had spotted another aged bowler playing, and he would start his bowling, making sure to play quite severely.

Eventually, he would contact the other bowler who would join him. And they would place a bet on the game.

Charlie made sure that he lost the first two games and would apologize to his opponent, saying that he could not understand why his game was so wrong. He would convince his opponent to play a third and final game for a wager much higher than the sum of the previous two games. Once they started, Charlie would revert to his usual game, which was very high standard. He would win very quickly, and his opponent would have no complaints because Charlie had told him that he was playing poorly and could play better. Charlie could encounter other bowlers and probably win three matches which more than paid for his day out. Life has a cruel way of showing us that we cannot take it for granted, and it shocked everyone when their only son Richard died. Charlie and Margaret were asleep in bed when the police informed them that they were needed at the hospital. Richard had gone into hospital for a minor operation to remove an abscess from his groin, spreading and killing him.

The funeral took place, and now Josephine was a widow, and she decided that the children could visit the grandparents, but she would cut them out of her life. A few years elapsed, and Margaret died, leaving Charlie in the house on his own.

Initially, the grandchildren would visit their grandfather often, but the visits became less frequent as the years passed.

Finally, in desperation, Charlie decided to visit his grandchildren and Josephine. They lived in a private house about ten miles away. Charlie was not sure of the house number, and it was only when one of the children spotted him outside that he was brought into the house. Remarkably Josephine, who had cut him out of her life, was very emotional. They embraced and agreed that bygones would be bygones. Charlie stayed for dinner and returned home that evening on the bus. The grandchildren took turns to check up on Grandad frequently.

Over the next few years, Charlie slowed down. His outdoor activities ceased. He was housebound, and his recreational activities consisted of gardening and walking to the pub.

However, he was always a welcome visitor to the pub. People respected Charlie because of his past reputation as a prize-fighter and his war service. However, Charlie retained all his faculties.

He was often invited to special local ceremonies to talk about his war career and the futility of war. It was late in his life that he realized that he was a very accomplished speaker, and his audience came from areas away from the village. He was an expert gardener, and he would show his carnations at local shows, and quite often, he would win first prize. Eventually, he was taken to hospital, where he died with some of his family beside him. One of his grandchildren held his hand as he passed away.

He was laid to rest with his wife Margaret, who was buried in the local cemetery. Later it was recognized that the grave was unmarked, and many of his relatives who lived in the USA could not find it. One of his grandchildren arranged a contribution from family members, and a beautiful marble headstone was erected.

THE END

IRISH MIKE

I f you are fortunate in life, you may meet a person with a natural charm who can over-come most obstacles and literally 'charm the birds from the trees' This is the story of the man we have called Irish Mike

Michael was born in Dublin, Ireland. He was the youngest child of the Quinn family and the last of ten children.

His brothers and sisters were all well-educated and respected members of the local fraternity. However, his mother was a devout Catholic, and all of the children had to attend home for the evening rosary. As the years passed, the rosary family members decreased until only he and his sister attended nightly.

The working of our almighty creator is truly re-markable because of resenting the imposition of this parental control; Mike would use this experience to his advantage very much in later life.

Mike was an incredibly gifted Irish patriot. To anyone knowing the Irish, this was a compliment of the highest order.

Unfortunately, he did not achieve the academic level of some of his brothers and sisters. Still, his innate sense of humor and honest opinion would always be a favorite amongst many admirers.

Mike decided to leave school at the age of 14 and started work as a farm laborer.

The open-air life suited him well, and his dealings with all the animals formed the basis of many of his ideas.

He told his mother that he would like to go to England and work in an office. With some surprise, his mother tried to persuade him to stay, but eventually, she could see that he was determined to flee from the nest and find his way in life.

Michael eventually obtained an office job in Liverpool, and he was swift to understand all the ramifications of office work.

At the age of 23, Michael passed the National Certificate in Commerce which was the next step in his career. He applied for a job with a leading car company and attended an interview at Speke Airport. He was successful in his application.

Michael arrived at the car company and was introduced to the company controller. After a short introduction, he was passed to his line supervisor and eventually his colleagues. He realized that he was in the Cost Accounting department and one of eight colleagues. Looking down the office, he estimated that the accounts department consisted of several sections with approximately 120 employees. Mike was an incredibly gifted Irish patriot.

To anyone knowing the Irish, this was a compliment of the highest order. Unfortunately, he did not achieve the academic level of some of his brothers and sisters. Still, his innate sense of humor and honest opinion would always be a favorite amongst many admirers. This environment was the opposite of the open-air life he had previously enjoyed. Still, surprisingly, he knew that this was the starting gate for his new career.

It took a little time to understand his new role,

but the local Liverpool sense of humor would be the forerunner for the rest of his life. He soon realized that Liverpool was a little Ireland without religion.

Initially, he was the object of the local satire, but as the days passed, he became the master of the art.

Everyone loved Michael. Amazingly there was a severe side to him which perplexed his colleagues. He had been working in his new job for several months, and his desk was situated adjacent to the typing pool.

He suddenly found that one of the typists was throwing paper clips onto his desk.

After a particularly heavy barrage of paperclips, he decided to talk to the girl and ask her not to throw any more paperclips. The girl named Sandra was one of seven typists, and most certainly, she was the prettiest. This encounter was the forerunner of a relationship.

Michael had a solid Catholic upbringing. This was the first girl he had dated without his mother knowing about it. On occasions, they would go to the swimming pool during the lunch hour, and occasionally they would come very close together at the end of the pool.

These meetings would stimulate Michael to swim away.

It was evident that Sandra was a siren at large. Their relationship lasted for several years, and Sandra taught Michael a lot about the opposite sex.

Unfortunately, Sandra was two-timing Michael and revealed that she thought that she was pregnant. Michael was shocked by this admission and immediately ended his association with Sandra.

Michael said that "he would pray for her," Two days later, she said, "that his prayers had been answered." He knew that he was not responsible for her problem and that his family would disown him if it had been confirmed.

Michael often spoke about 'the little people. He was, of course, referring to the fairies who lived in the hedgerows in Ireland. Without a doubt, all his colleagues loved him, but this belief was a joke that they could not understand. People would often challenge him on this belief, and the herd instinct was massing in the entire office.

Finally, this situation reached the Controller, and he called Michael into his office to understand the problem better. Michael was in the Controller's office for approximately one hour. At the end of the meeting, he realized that Michael was deadly serious in his belief.

The Controller addressed the whole office and said that we all have our own beliefs and must respect others even though we disagree. Michael was now liberated but decided to talk less freely on the subject.

On certain occasions when the workday had finished, and some of the offices had retired to the pub, the fairy's story would surface, and Michael would explain graphically how his friends had helped him. Perhaps one of his favorite tales was his first meeting with a fairy on the golf course.

Michael had shanked his golf shot into a smooth patch close to the hedgerows. He was about to take his swing when he heard a voice pleading with him not to take a divot because this would damage the center green of the fairy village.

The fairy promised Michael that he would grant

him a favor if he moved his ball away from the patch and replaced it with another place. Michael would win the next primary golf contest that he played.

The following primary upcoming contest was the Captain's Open Day, and Michael won it by five shots. During this story, one of the members in the pub was about to take a large drink of his beer. However, unable to control his laughter, he duly sprayed the contents of his mouth over several of his colleagues.

Back in the office, Michael's work was always of a very high standard. However, he had one major fault, and that was timekeeping. It was not un-usual for him to turn up for work late. Often, he could be as late as one hour.

Michaels immediate supervisor warned him that things had to change, or else? Later that day, Michael handed his supervisor a notice to quit, with immediate effect.

Arriving back at home, he realized that he had acted impulsively, but he had no regrets. Instead, he bought the local paper and scanned the job va-cancies section.

One of the adverts that caught his attention was for a position at a local Airport. He applied for the vacancy, and after the interview, he immediately got the position.

In the first few weeks, he realized that the most crucial aspect of Airport life was controlling time, and he was determined to obey these rules.

During lunchtime breaks, he would wander around the various buildings and hangars. One day, as Michael took a walk during the lunch hour, he spotted a female coming through the arrivals.

She was wearing a long grey coat, and their eyes met, it was love at first sight, without hesitation, he reached out and carried her heavy suitcase towards the taxi stand.

The latest plane arrival had used all available taxis. However, Michael knew that life had predestined this meeting, and he escorted the lady to his car. "Where can I take you, my good lady," he asked.

She replied, "Hopefully this is, not a kidnap, so Broadgreen if you don't mind."

Michael introduced himself, and she responded by saying, "my name is Grace."

As they started a conversation, he was 'eyeing her over.' He thought he liked very much what he saw. When they arrived at their destination, he asked her whether he could meet with her again soon.

Grace replied that she usually visited a dance hall with girlfriends in Southport on a Saturday night, and they could meet there.

On the weekend, Michael and a couple of male friends arrived at a public house adjacent to the ballroom. They enjoyed a few pints before walking across to the ballroom.

A dance was in session, and the ballroom lights now dimmed, which set a perfect intimate scene. The men stood on one side of the ballroom, and the women stood on the opposite side. Michael scanned the far side, and as he spotted Grace, some fellow picked her up for a dance.

He watched as she danced with the man and wondered was this competition or something was even worse. At the announcement of the next dance, Michael crossed the floor and asked Grace for a dance.

Typically, first meetings are non-events, but

Michael knew that this time was more than a chance meeting. He had bragged before that the girl he would marry would be Irish, a nurse, and a snug fit on the dance floor. So his first question to Grace was, "what do you do for a living" and the reply was, "I am a nurse at the hospital."

When the first dance was over, Michael remained with Grace. They interrogated each other about general life events and current positions.

It was rather interesting that both Irish-born should meet in England. Towards the end of the evening, Michael told Grace that he had traveled in his friend's Humber Hawk car, and it would be no trouble to drop her off in Broadgreen. Grace agreed and spoke to her friends, telling them that she was traveling back with the man she had been dancing with all evening.

Arriving back at Broadgreen, Michael had already made his next date to meet up outside the hospital at 6.30 pm the following Wednesday.

The months passed, and the couple met on every possible occasion, including meeting to introduce both sides of the families.

Michael had progressed very well at the Airport and had achieved various promotions. He now had a senior management position and announced his wish to learn how to pilot a plane.

It took a few months of dedicated work to master the art of flying a plane.

Still, he applied for his pilot's license and sat the various tests before being rewarded with a license. His first few flights were local, including Birmingham, London, and Glasgow. Grace was very proud of her boyfriend.

Michael was a carefree, happy, go-lucky person while Grace was thinking about the future. The couple met at their favorite coffee shop, and Grace said to Michael that she thought it

would be good to take a break from the routine and stay apart for three weeks. Michael disagreed and said that he would give it a try.

After the break, the couple met again in Dale Street in Liverpool. Michael was walking slightly ahead of Grace when she confessed that a future apart was not a good idea. Michael's immediate response was, "Why don't you marry me then." (On reflection, it could be said that this response could have been better.)

Grace immediately replied YES. Both parties were now one, and their future together was assured.

While they were in Liverpool, they visited some jewelers' shops, and Grace eventually decided on an engagement ring. The wedding took place in Dublin, and the priest who married them was Grace's uncle.

Michael had prepared his speech, but he was not satisfied with the result. Later the couple flew from Dublin to Heathrow before traveling to Spain, where they spent two beautiful weeks. Returning to England meant that nest-building had to begin. Initially, rented accommodation was necessary, but the time arrived when a home of their own was required.

After a few months, Grace and Michael found a very modern house which meant that both had to change their jobs to ensure the approval of the sale. Grace had no problem because the new hospital was much closer to home than previously.

Michael was fortunate enough to arrange an internal transfer with the same airline.

Grace spent months furnishing the house and Michael sorting out the overgrown garden. Finally, after two years, a baby boy was born, and they named him Cedric. Michael realized that he was now a solid married man and father.

Late one evening in November, he was traveling the main highway home. Traveling at a speed of 60 miles per hour, he came to a slight rise in the road. He could see about 500 yards, and he noticed a vehicle on the left side of the roadway. He noticed that fog seemed to be little more than a haze in the dip of the road. He traveled onwards in the fast lane when he realized that the vehicle was, in fact, a lorry and trailer. The lorry and trailer completely blocked both the slow and fast lanes. Immediately Michael realized that, barring a miracle, he was going to crash into the trailer.

Pulling his car hard to the left, he managed to avoid the trailer. Still, his car skidded and hit a raised central reservation, immediately rebounding back towards the slow lane. A car coming along the slow lane hit his car, knocking him out of the vehicle onto the roadway.

Michael was later told that he was taken by ambulance.

A day later, he could phone Grace from the hospital bed to tell her that he was ok but kept in the hospital for an X-ray and further observation.

Michael's recovery was slow. When he was eventually released from the hospital, he decided that he had a lot of work to do with his body and return to full fitness. He was advised to take up martial arts exercises.

Initially, Michael found the work a bore, but as the weeks passed, he noticed gradual improvements to his physique, and subsequently, he was in the best shape for years.

The following year Grace gave birth to a baby girl whom they named Nora. Then, reflecting on the current situation, they decided to take a holiday to Australia.

They arranged to spend time traveling part-time and staying with relatives.

On one of the trips, they decided to abandon the

car and look at one of the waterfalls.

Just ahead of them was a lady who was speaking to her husband. The lady lost her footing and crashed through some flimsy fencing.

She then fell over 30 feet into a pool at the bottom of the falls. In an instant, Michael discarded his shoes and most of his clothes. He quickly got over the fence and dropped to her aid. The woman was a non-swimmer, and she was terrified.

Michael slowly moved her downstream to a safer place where the fire brigade and ambulance could rescue her and take her to the hospital.

Michael became an instant celebrity and figured in all the Australian papers. When Grace was interviewed and asked about her husband's rescue action she replied, "he is always doing that kind of thing."

The holiday ended far too quickly, and they returned home to carry on where they left off. Today the family is still united, and the children are successful adults.

THE END

About The Author

Hugh, author of The Incredible Geezer is a professional and family man. He married Grace and together they raised a beautiful family.

As a Management Accountant for a multi-national company, Hugh had the opportunity to work in several countries, including Portugal, Brazil, and Italy, for long periods.

His engagements and experiences in these countries continue to inspire his writing.